For the children of Hawai‘i

Also published by Ruwanga Trading:

The Goodnight Gecko
The Whale Who Wanted to be Small
The Wonderful Journey
A Whale's Tale
The Gift of Aloha
The Shark Who Learned a Lesson
Gecko Hide and Seek
The Brave Little Turtle
Tikki Turtle's Quest
How the Geckos Learned to Chirp

First published 2009 by Ruwanga Trading
ISBN 978-0970152817
Printed in China by Everbest Printing Co., Ltd

BOOK ENQUIRIES AND ORDERS:
Booklines Hawaii, a division of The Islander Group
269 Pali'i Street
Mililani, Hawaii 96789
Phone: 808-676-0116, ext.206
Fax: 808-676-5156
Toll Free: 1-877-828-4852
Website: www.islandergroup.com

Happy as a Dolphin

A child's celebration of Hawai'i

Written and illustrated by Gill McBarnet

I'm as happy as a dolphin
Jumping from a wave,
As shy as a spotted eel
Hiding in his cave.

I'm as dainty as a ghost crab
Tip-toe-ing on the sand,
And free as a seabird
Skimming sea and land.

I'm as big as a mighty whale
Powered by his tail
And small as a hermit crab
Creeping like a snail.

I'm as peaceful as a moon jelly
Drifting by with ease,
And delicate as the coral reef
Branching out like trees.

I'm as brave as a diver,
diving deep, you see …
And careful as the little fish
Who dart and quickly flee!

I'm as friendly as a palm tree
Waving in the breeze,
And graceful as a hula dancer
Swaying arms and knees.

I'm as wistful as the chanter
Blowing on his conch,
And solemn as the steady drum –
a haunting, ancient hum.

I'm as nimble as my fingers

   Threading flowers one by one,

And sweet as the fragrance

   Of a lei that's newly hung.

I'm as proud as a rodeo rider
"Watch me, if you please!"
And timid as a little mouse
Peeping through the leaves.

I'm as cuddly as a newborn lamb
In rolling pastures green,
And shiny as a dewdrop
On flowers that brightly gleam.

I'm as lazy as a lizard
Dozing where it's sunny,
As busy as the buzzy bees
Making golden honey.

I'm as tall as a mountain peak
   With valleys green and steep,
And fresh as the river
   Filling pools so cool and deep.

I'm excited like the mynah birds
Chattering in the trees,
And snug in my little house
So cosy in the breeze.

I'm as rosy as the sunset
of warm color glows,
And bright as the tip of sun
Before it dips and goes.

And when at night
we turn out the light,
I'm as quiet as the moon up high…

and I'm soon asleep like baby Kai

...with the ocean

lullaby.